A TEMPLAR BOOK

Produced by The Templar Company plc,
Pippbrook Mill, London Road, Dorking, Surrey RH4 1JE, Great Britain.

Text copyright © *Jumbo Saves the Day* 1952 by Darrell Waters Limited
Illustration and design copyright © 1994 by The Templar Company plc
Enid Blyton is a registered trademark of Darrell Waters Limited

This edition produced for Parragon Books,
Unit 13-17, Avonbridge Trading Estate, Atlantic Road, Avonmouth, Bristol BS11 9Q

This book contains material first published as
Good Old Jumbo in My First Enid Blyton Book
by Latimer House Limited, 1952.

Illustrated by Maggie Downer

Printed and bound in Italy

ISBN 1 85813 548 6

Enid Blyton's

POCKET LIBRARY

JUMBO
SAVES THE DAY

Illustrated by Maggie Downer

PARRAGON

Outside the playroom window, inside an old flower-pot, lived three small pixies called Briar, Berry and Buttercup. The toys knew them very well indeed, for the pixies often came into the playroom at night when it was dark, and played with them.

Briar and Berry were big strong pixies, but Buttercup was small and sweet. She was their sister, and they loved her very much. All the toys loved her too, and they let her ride in the wooden train, and the toy motor car, and even on the big rocking-horse as many times as she liked.

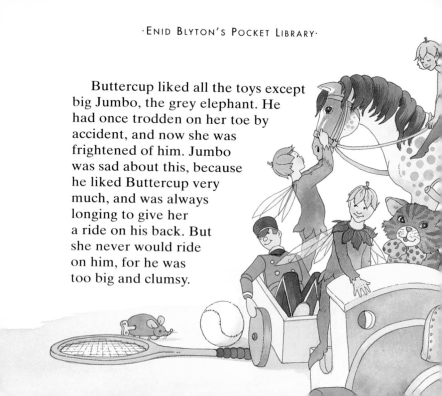

Buttercup liked all the toys except big Jumbo, the grey elephant. He had once trodden on her toe by accident, and now she was frightened of him. Jumbo was sad about this, because he liked Buttercup very much, and was always longing to give her a ride on his back. But she never would ride on him, for he was too big and clumsy.

The toys belonged to two children called Amy and Andrew, but lately the children hadn't bothered to play with their toys very often. Their Uncle Jim had given them something they liked much better – two pairs of roller skates! You should have seen how the two children tore round and round on them! Goodness, they went like lightning!

The toys were jealous of the roller skates. The children kept them in the toy cupboard but every night the toys pushed them out.

"They are nasty things," said the clockwork clown, giving the skates a push. "I don't know why the children like them better than they like us. Get out of the toy cupboard, you ugly things! You don't belong in here!"

Then, bump-bump! Out would tumble the four skates on to the floor. They weren't alive, so they didn't mind one way or another. But the children were always puzzled to know how it was their skates fell out of the toy cupboard so often!

So every night the toys were very glad when the three pixies came to join them.

"It's nice to have *somebody* to play with," said the teddy bear. "The children hardly ever take any notice of us now!"

Then one night Berry and Briar came in through the window in a great hurry, looking as scared as could be.

"Toys, toys! Whatever shall we do? Six naughty red goblins came tonight and stole away Buttercup, our little pixie sister! Oh, whatever shall we do?"

The toys turned pale with fright. Even the teddy bear, who was the bravest of all of them, looked quite white, so you can guess how frightened they all were. No one liked the red goblins.

They were very naughty and liked nothing better than to play nasty tricks on people. They had once poured glue all over the playroom window-sill in the hope that one of the toys would get stuck there. Another time they had stolen pieces from all the children's jigsaws so that none could be finished completely. And now they had taken away Buttercup! Whatever could be done?

"They'll have taken her back to Goblin Land!" said the panda. "That's a long way from here!"

"Well, you can't ask *me* to go after them," said the clockwork train, in a hurry. "I can only run on my rails."

"And my key is lost," said the clockwork motor car. "*I* can't go!"

"Nobody wants to go!" wailed the two pixies sorrowfully. "Poor Buttercup! She'll never come back again." Then the big elephant, Jumbo, spoke up in his big deep voice.

"*I* will go and chase those goblins!" he said.
"I'm not afraid!"

"Dear old Jumbo!" cried all the toys
together. "What a kind, brave elephant
you are! But you're so slow and
clumsy it would take you
ages to get there."

"Ah, but I've got a splendid idea!" said Jumbo. "I want you to strap those roller skates on to my big feet. Then, if you'll help me to practise, I shall go like the wind, roller-skating down the paths to Goblin Land!"

Well, what an idea! Did you ever hear anything like it! An elephant on roller skates! Anyway, you should have seen how the toys and the two pixies clapped their hands when they heard what Jumbo said. They thought it was the best idea they had ever heard.

"Quick! Get the roller skates!" cried Berry.

"Where are they?" cried Briar.

Panda got one, Teddy found another, and the two biggest dolls brought the last two.

Then they strapped them on to Jumbo's big, clumsy feet. He *did* look funny!

"I'm just going to have a skate round the playroom to see if I can do it properly," said Jumbo, shaking with excitement. And off he went, round and round the room.

Crash! Crash! Crash! went his feet, as he tried his hardest to skate with all four at once. Dear me, you should have seen him!

All the toys got out of his way in a great hurry, for his four feet shot out all over the place, and he didn't know at all where he was going. He knocked the clockwork clown flat on his nose and ran over the teddy bear's big toe. Goodness, it was a sight to see!

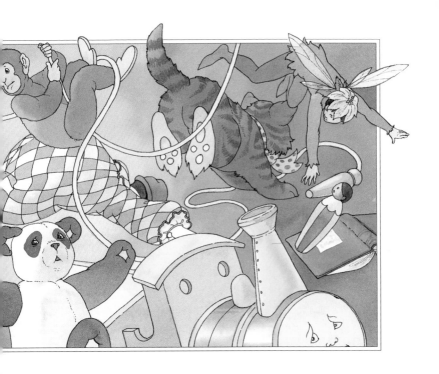

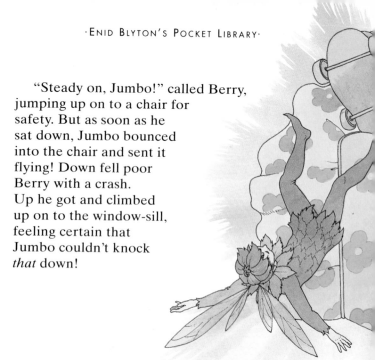

"Steady on, Jumbo!" called Berry, jumping up on to a chair for safety. But as soon as he sat down, Jumbo bounced into the chair and sent it flying! Down fell poor Berry with a crash. Up he got and climbed up on to the window-sill, feeling certain that Jumbo couldn't knock *that* down!

After a little while Jumbo began to skate much better. His legs went properly and he found that he could skate right round the nursery and back again without falling over once. He did feel proud.

"Now I'm ready to go after Buttercup and the goblins," he said to the pixies. "Jump up on my back and tell me the right way to go."

So Berry and Briar jumped up on to his broad back, and hung on tightly. Crash! Crash! Crash! went the roller skates as Jumbo skated out of the room and down the passage that led to the garden. What a noise he made! It's a wonder he didn't wake the whole house up!

Berry and Briar soon managed
to unlock the back door and
the three of them slipped
out into the garden.
The moon was shining
brightly as Jumbo went
skating splendidly
down the garden
path.

If one of his feet slipped he still had three others to help him, so he didn't fall over at all.

He *did* go at a rate! Out into the lane he skated and over the hill, until he came to the extra-large rabbit-hole that was the entrance to Goblin Land.

The streets of Goblin Land are very straight and smooth, so soon Jumbo found he could go even faster! Crash! Crash! Crash! went his skates and he tore along faster than any motor car could possibly go. Berry and Briar soon lost their hats, for the wind streamed past them and snatched away their hats with greedy fingers.

"There they are, there they are!"
shouted Berry suddenly, so loudly
that he frightened Briar and nearly
made him fall off Jumbo's back.
Jumbo looked in front of him
and saw, far in the distance,
a crowd of little red goblins
riding yellow rocking-horses.
One of them held Buttercup
tightly in his arms, whilst
he shouted to his
rocking-horse to
rock faster and
faster through
Goblin Land.

Jumbo made a sound like a trumpet and skated on faster than ever. The goblins heard the crash of his skates and looked back. When they saw Jumbo roller-skating behind them, carrying Berry and Briar on his back, they could hardly believe their eyes. They shouted loudly to their rocking-horses.

"Go on! Go on! You must go faster still! Hurry, hurry, hurry!"

The rocking-horses rocked away till it seemed as if they must tumble on their noses or tails. They went very fast indeed. But Jumbo went even faster. How he skated! You could hardly see his legs moving, they went so quickly.

"They're taking Buttercup to the Deep Green Cave!" cried Berry suddenly. "Oh dear, catch them before they get there, Jumbo, or we shall never see our dear little sister again!"

Sure enough,
they were heading
straight for the Deep
Green Cave, the place
where all the goblins'
nastiest magic is made. Jumbo
skated even faster to get there
before the goblins did – and he got
there with just a single second to spare.

Now luckily, Jumbo was so big that
he easily blocked the entrance to the
Deep Green Cave. And as the
first goblin came rocking
towards him, Jumbo
scooped him up in
his big long trunk
and left him dangling
in the branches of a
nearby tree.

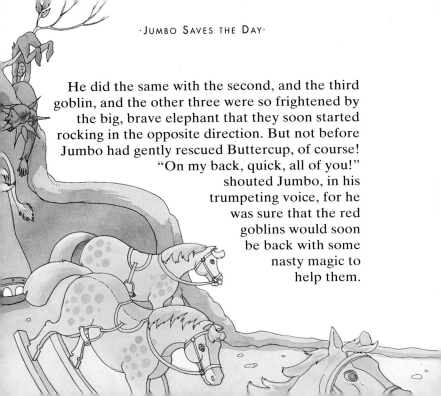

He did the same with the second, and the third
goblin, and the other three were so frightened by
the big, brave elephant that they soon started
rocking in the opposite direction. But not before
Jumbo had gently rescued Buttercup, of course!
"On my back, quick, all of you!"
shouted Jumbo, in his
trumpeting voice, for he
was sure that the red
goblins would soon
be back with some
nasty magic to
help them.

Berry jumped up. Then it was Buttercup's turn. She had quite forgotten that she had said she never, ever would ride on Jumbo's back so she got up as quickly as ever she could, and Briar followed close behind her.

Then back went Jumbo through Goblin Land,
skating as fast as his four legs would carry him.
Long before the red goblins came running after
them, Jumbo was out of sight, crash-crash-
crashing along on his four roller skates!
It didn't take him long to
get back to the playroom,
very much out of breath,
but simply delighted that
Buttercup was safely home
again. The toys gave him a
great welcome, and cheered
him with all their might.
His trunk blushed quite
red with pride.

The toys unstrapped the skates from his tired feet and put them away again. Then they heard the first cock crowing to say that day was coming, so they hurriedly said goodbye to the pixies and climbed back into the toy cupboard to go to sleep.

Berry and Briar patted Jumbo before they went, but Buttercup flung her arms round his trunk and kissed him lovingly.

"You're a dear, brave Jumbo," she said, "and I'm sorry I ever said you were clumsy. I'll come and ride on you every single night if you'll let me!"

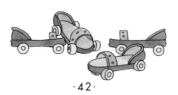

Then off she went, and left Jumbo standing by himself, very happy indeed. And he was happier still the night after, for Buttercup came back and kept her promise. Good old Jumbo carried her all around the nursery and she wasn't frightened at all, no, not even for a minute!